Ten at the Wedding

Stories by Lynn Jatania

Kitty-Corner Publishing
Ontario, Canada

Publisher's Note: This is a work of fiction. Names, characters, places, and incidents are a product of the author's imagination. Locales and public names are sometimes used for atmospheric purposes. Any resemblance to actual people, living or dead, or to businesses, companies, events, institutions, or locales is completely coincidental.

Book Layout © 2017 BookDesignTemplates.com
Editing by Morning Rain Publishing
Cover design by Blend Creations

Ten at the Wedding/ Lynn Jatania. -- 1st ed.
ISBN 978-1-7751233-0-9

For Neel

at the wedding

Lisa at the Wedding

Click.

Lisa sees the world through a tiny glass window with a black border. The little circle in the middle lets her know if she's in focus.

But she's always focused.

Click-click-click.

Her finger presses too hard on the shutter, taking multiple images at once. The bride smiles, slowly, her glass lifting for yet another toast, frame by frame like pages in a flip book.

It's out there, somewhere. The shot. Lisa knows it, but she's afraid the moment is gone, and she's missed it. It's her first wedding, and the pressure of capturing the details of a live event—each second so fleeting, the light ever changing—is huge. This is nothing like babies in her studio, snuggled up and quiet, or family photo shoots on nature trails when a few candies in her pocket will buy her all the do-overs she needs. She's grown accustomed to that level of control: the confidence of knowing that no matter what, she's going to get it. The shot.

It's the one that captures not just a perfect moment in time, but souls and spirits, too. A real moment, natural with emotion and love and light, posed yet not posed. A whole life inside four inches by six inches. It's a lot to ask of a few pixels and a scrap of paper, she knows, but she also believes it can be done. There is magic inside this lens.

It's getting late, and Lisa snaps away, looking outside the head table for the shot. Her pictures of the ceremony turned out well—she had a peek in the car on the way over—and the weather cooperated for the formal photo shoot afterwards. She couldn't have asked for more, and yet, she knows it still eludes her, doesn't live on her camera's memory card quite yet. Will it be the minister, aging in his traditional collar, blue eyes sparking as he sneaks a nip of champagne? Will it be the one young lady hanging at the back, too shy to enter the fray as the bouquet is thrown, but too superstitious not to at least stand nearby with a hopeful look on her face? Will it be the lady in the fabulous hat—the groom's aunt, she overheard someone say—purple and brimmed wide enough to block the view of every table behind her? Lisa snaps and chimps, looking at the viewfinder after each shot, an amateur move to see what she's captured. *Come on, come on, you're better than that*, she thinks.

Earlier that afternoon, she'd thought she'd captured it. It was in the garden behind the church. A lovely spot with the perfect mix of sun and shade, flowering shrubs for the serious poses, and a little creek down at the very back for some whimsical pics of the bridesmaids and groomsmen hamming it up. She'd finished up the family shots, and most of the guests had left off to a pub up the street to kill time watching a baseball game until the reception. The bride had gone inside with her entourage for a pee break, and Lisa sat on the grass to change to the wide-angle lens, getting ready for a few last distance shots of the bride and groom on the little bridge over the creek.

She'd taken the camera apart and pulled out the new lens when she noticed the flower girl, sitting alone, picking through the lawn with the care of an archeologist on a dig, the pink poof of her dress against the dark brown of her skin making her the prettiest flower in the garden.

"Lose something?" Lisa asked.

The girl shook her head, her crown of roses slipping to one side. "I'm looking for a four-leaf clover. Miss Hamilton says they're lucky."

"Oh, I see. Want some help?"

"Yup." The little girl nodded. Lisa sat her camera down and dutifully started combing through the clovers hiding in the tall grass.

"What's your name?" Lisa asked.

"Ella," she said. "If you find one, you can make a wish and then you can get anything you want."

"And what is it that you want, Ella?"

"A new horse for my Barbie. I have one, but it's brown, and Brooklynn has a white one with pink hair, and you can braid the hair and put a ribbon on it, and that one is better."

Lisa smiled. *Oh, for the days when a white Barbie horse was your greatest wish.*

Ella pulled a clover from the ground excitedly, then frowned and tossed it aside, rejected as not wish worthy. *Even her frown is adorable,* Lisa thought. *What is she, five, maybe six? Daisy would be the same age around now, if only, if only.*

Ella squinted up at Lisa. "Want to come over to my house and play?"

"Oh, I think I'll be too busy. I'm working." In explanation, she picked up her camera, still naked on the front, and began to fit the new lens in place.

"Maybe your girl can come over, then?" Ella asked with the confidence of knowing that every family matches her own, every lady has a little girl.

Lisa shook her head and swallowed. "No, I don't have any kids."

"Oh. Okay."

They sat together in silence, Lisa giving a wry smile, lifting her face to the sun, letting its heat warm her again. She finally snapped the new lens in place and aimed it out at the landscape, taking a test shot of the entire garden.

"Don't forget to look," reminded Ella.

Lisa nodded and put the camera in her right hand so she could smooth the greens on her left. *Clover beds are always so soft,* she thought, her mind drifting. *Velvety and soothing.*

Suddenly, it popped out. Four leaves, right under her hand. She plucked it from the ground and held it out to Ella, whose eyes widened as she squealed in delight. She snatched up the clover and held it coquettishly to her cheek, experienced with years of photo-shoot ready smart phones.

"Take my picture?" she asked.

It was the wrong lens entirely for this portrait, but she couldn't resist. Sometimes you choose the moment, sometimes the moment chooses you. She held the camera up to her eye and clicked.

Achingly close. But not quite.

❧

The cake has been served. As Lisa walks by the dessert table, the waft of sugar and chocolate remind her she hasn't eaten all day, but she'll take a break after she has it. The dancing is about to begin, and she hates to use the flash; she knows she'll never get that soft, lived-in look she loves for her work in the glare of white light. There's just enough late summer sun filtering in through the big picture windows for one or two orange-tinged pictures of the first dance.

The groom sweeps the bride around him in a grand gesture, her big white skirt flaring as she spins into his arms, and they jive and swing to the upbeat tune, faces glowing. Lisa clicks but can only ever catch one face, one smile as one turns forward and one turns away. Nothing that captures the togetherness of this moment, the warmth of the sunset, the goodwill of the guests.

Ella runs onto the dance floor, whooping, "I love this song!" She twirls and twirls, the crowd laughing, the bride and groom pausing, delighted to share the spotlight. The groom scoops Ella up in his arms, and Lisa realizes she doesn't know who Ella is. Perhaps a cousin, perhaps a niece. No matter, because the three of them are laughing, man, woman, and child, and they are happy, happy, and Lisa clicks the camera one last time.

Charity at the Wedding

7:02 a.m.

Charity rolls over, awake on her own for the first time in memory, no little fingers prodding her to consciousness. She instinctively gropes in the basement gloom for the phone on her bedside table, clicking to check her mail even though she knows it's unlikely they would have sent anything overnight.

Her inbox is empty. The acceptances should have been out yesterday, but still nothing. She can't decide if no news is good or bad. She's leaning towards bad but forcing herself to remain hopeful for one very important reason.

A dark, coily head of hair appears at the end of the bed, two big brown eyes barely able to peer over the edge of the mattress. Ella blinks sleep out of her eyes.

"Mommy, can I put my dress on right now?" she whispers.

"Sure, baby. Sure."

❦

8:15 a.m.

Charity is preparing herself a feta cheese omelet—the cheese scored on sale at the market, one day past its expiry date, the grocer with the kind eyes slipping it quietly into her basket when she came in. Ella is eating a bowl of Cheerios in her poof of a pink dress; Charity still hasn't figured out how to attach the ring of roses to her hair. She's chattering away overtop of a mermaid cartoon on the TV. "And Miss Hamilton says that I can have the biggest piece of cake, bigger than everyone else, and from the corner, too, with extra icing. Miss Hamilton says it is going to be a chocolate cake, and chocolate is the best, but also I will be very careful with my dress because you have to be careful with it, like I am being careful right now."

Charity slips the omelet onto a plate—perfectly cooked, she can smell the sage—then taps her phone with one hand as she carries the food to the table. Still no messages, and she is no longer hungry.

"You know, when you go back to school next year you might have to call Miss Hamilton by a new name. Some ladies change their last names when they get married."

Ella's eyes go wide. "What will I call her?"

"Missus..." Charity casts about and comes up with nothing. "Well, Missus something." She should probably dig out the invitation before the wedding and figure out some names, try to put a little effort into being a good guest even if she's only coming along as the flower girl's plus one.

Ella frowns. "I do not like that."

Charity grins. She wonders, not for the first time, whether they gave her the right baby at the hospital. Ella is so sure of herself, so different from her mother outside and in. *Must get it from her father*, Charity supposes, *that and her dark looks.*

"Should we boycott the wedding in protest?"

"What's... bloy-clot?"

"Skip the whole thing. Let them know we won't take this name-change nonsense lying down."

Ella's mouth hangs open, and Charity laughs. "Don't worry, baby, we'll go. We'll go."

❧

3:30 p.m.

Charity paces back and forth on the small terrace behind the church. Still no messages, and she's decided there must have been some mistake. There's probably no one there on a Saturday, but she has to call anyway, has to feel like she's doing something. She brings her cell phone to her ear.

What she wouldn't give for a cigarette right now, even though it's been months since she had a craving.

Ella seems happy enough sitting in the grass, chattering away to the photographer as she swaps out her camera lens. Ella is everyone's friend, and Charity wishes she could freeze time, freeze this moment, and never have Ella learn how the world really works. Charity's relieved Ella made it through the ceremony without getting anything on the pretty pink dress, all the little pearl buttons around the neckline intact, and Charity doesn't care what happens now. She can use the dress to play at the park or for dress-up or anything she wants. Grass stains? Sure, whatever.

The cell phone rings and rings in her ear. Who doesn't have voicemail in this day and age? Charity listens to it, ring, ring, ring, chewing on a thumbnail as she looks out past Ella to where the bride and groom are posing on a little bridge over a stream. Ella's teacher giggles as her new husband playacts at tossing her in the water. Charity hopes this isn't the secret to happiness. She's given up on men for real this time—enough of moving Ella around from guy to guy. It's just the two of them now—pretty pink dresses but no veils, no white, no groom.

She looks at her daughter and knows it's time to stop just existing. It is time to create a life. No more waitressing, strawberry picking, selling flowers on street corners. No more moving Ella in and out of her mother's house as she tries one new venture after another. Ella has friends, a school she loves, and Charity swears they are staying put this time, even if it is in that goddamn damp basement apartment.

This time. This is the one.

"Hello, you've reached the admissions office at the Lincoln Culinary Institute. We can't take your call right now, but if you leave a message we will respond within two working days."

Charity hangs up before the beep.

&

7:30 p.m.

Charity picks at her meal. As usual, for an event like this, the vegetarian option consists of an extra helping of all side dishes. By habit, she reforms the meal in her mind, adding a little Gruyère and some caramelized onions, maybe some parsnips to turn the boiled potatoes and carrots into a proper main course mash. She sighs, as well as she can, since there's not much breathing space at this back-corner table, pinned up against the wall like an afterthought. At least Ella seems to be doing well at the head table, the bridesmaids all buzzing around her, cooing and petting her hair. Charity fidgets with the scarf she's fashioned as a belt to cover a mystery stain on her dress, trying to keep her hands busy.

There's an older lady sitting next to her, Olive something, in an enormous purple hat. She blocks the view of the podium as she prattles on, dominating the view and the conversation.

"Of course, my tastes do tend to be different than most, but I will say that my nephew's wedding, which was in France—her people are from France—was at a chateau, and if one can have a wedding at a chateau, then naturally, one should. Certainly, France does have a lot of chateaus, which does help."

Charity tries to make a noncommittal and unencouraging noise, but it's more than enough to keep the conversation alive.

"Of course, he turned out to be a bit of a shiftless scalawag, if you ask me. Black sheep of the family and all that. Burned through his poor wife's inheritance— they're from money, old money—or at least, they were. Never could buckle down and make something of himself." The older lady sniffs, takes a sip of her wine, then gives it a disappointed frown. "I suppose some people take the Life of Leisure idea far too literally."

Everyone else at the table, Charity notices, has suddenly become very interested in their entrees. Olive has begun addressing her directly.

"It must be nice, don't you think, to have all your dreams handed to you, with no effort at all, and to be able to treat them with such casual disregard that you can throw them away like a used tissue?"

Olive pauses expectantly, while Charity shakes her head, more unable to speak than truly disagree. She thinks that having a few dreams handed to her sounds pretty good right about now.

"Well, you're a wiser girl than him, then, because real dreams, the good ones, can't be delivered like a package you forgot you ordered. They take a little elbow grease. They take a little passion. They take a little dedication!" She reaches a crescendo with her finger in the air.

The phone bings, and Charity grabs for it, worming her way out of her seat without even bothering to make an excuse. She dashes across the wooden dance floor in the centre of the ring of tables, out through the main doors to the hallway. Eagerly she pulls up her mail, desperate to know, not wanting to know, already knowing.

But it's only a note from her mother reminding her that toilet paper is on sale at the pharmacy tomorrow.

She returns to the table, wedging herself back in, finding that her picked-over food is gone. She's surrounded by the backs of everyone's heads as they turn to listen to a toast by the best man. Tears prick her eyes, and she feels a gentle hand on her arm.

"Something the matter, dear?"

Charity looks up at Olive. Her mouth opens, but she knows one word will become a sob all too easily.

Olive nods, the brim of her purple hat dipping up and down. "I see you, you know. I can tell by the look in your eyes. You are ready for greatness." She gestures at the head table. "Why is happiness so easy for some and not others? I could write a book on the subject." She sighs, then smiles. "You, though, I have a good feeling about. You've got spirit."

Olive nods once, as if it's all decided. "You're going to be just fine."

She digs in her purse and comes up with a caramel wrapped in crinkly cellophane. "Candy?"

Charity nods and takes the treat, its sweetness filling her mouth. Ella has run onto the dance floor and is twirling to the music, skirt spinning about her, like the petals of a flower. *She is happy,* Charity thinks. *She is happy.*

Maybe the best dreams really are delivered to your door, just like that, like a package you forgot you ordered.

Charity gets to her feet and dances out to join Ella, hands in the air, her phone left facedown on the table.

Tim at the Wedding

im sits at the Table of Singles, unable to get comfortable on the upright metal chair. He's got his standard conversation points ready to go: friend of the groom from high school, works as a computer programmer, yes, the weather is unseasonably warm for this time of year. But right now, he's stuck between a couple of empty chairs, smiling like an idiot at the general crowd, feeling out of place.

"You look like you're out of time," she says as she plonks down next to him, sloshing her pink cocktail a bit as she sets it on the table.

Tim startles and resists the urge to look back and forth to make sure she's talking to him.

"Pardon me?"

She reaches over and straightens his bow tie. "No offense, or anything. I like it. You've got a real sweet

Donald O'Connor, *Anything Goes* kind of thing going on."

Tim stammers, "Um, well, it's supposed to be more of a *Doctor Who* thing, but um, thanks. You like old movies?" He should have guessed. Her shiny gold dress is vintage, her hair sweeping over one eye in short, old-fashioned waves, like a publicity shot of a young Liz Taylor he saw once, if Liz were Asian.

"Oh, I watch as much as I can—used to watch more as a kid, with my parents. It's how they learned English. But now, I mean, there's just so much out there. New stuff flying in your face all the time, you know? Like, Jack Lemmon is awesome, but Woody Allen is awesome, and Soderburgh is awesome. You just try to drink it all in, right?"

Tim nods and grins, his cheeks stretching beyond his usual polite half-smile. He takes a swig of his wine. "So, tell me, what's your favourite film?" he says into his glass.

She snorts. "As if I could choose one. It's like choosing your favourite jellybean from a ten-pound bag. Sometimes I like raspberry, some days I'm in the mood for lemon. And sometimes, you pull out a big juicy green one, and you think, ugh, watermelon, and then it turns out to be tropical punch and mmm."

She takes a big sip of her drink and thanks the server as he puts a plate of food in front of her before going on.

"Now, if you pressure me..." She pauses and looks him in the eye. "Are you pressuring me?"

Tim feels his stomach flip, like he's being interrogated for a crime he didn't commit. Is he supposed to respond? "Um... yes?"

"Well then, alright. I usually say *All About Eve* because it's the highbrow answer. You've seen it?"

"I think once, in university."

"Great. Bette Davis is just so wonderful, you know? 'Fasten your seatbelts,' and all that. But really, if you really, really want to know... do you really want to know?"

Yes, he does. He's pretty sure he does. She scoops up her drink and leans in for the reveal as Tim leans back, imagining a big pink splotch appearing on his white dinner jacket. He can smell cherries on her breath.

"It's *Easter Parade*." She sits back, waiting for a reaction.

Tim gives a little shake of his head. "I'm afraid I don't know much about musicals."

She snorts again. An oddly lovely sound, Tim finds.

"Oh, don't tell me you don't love them, too, you with your Danny Kaye hair. You can't tell me you don't watch *Easter Parade* every year when it's on." She reaches over to his plate with her knife and fork. "Is that the chicken you've got? Mind if I try some?" she says, not waiting for approval before cutting herself a piece.

Tim gives her a wry smile. "I think I saw *Mary Poppins* once as a kid," he offers.

"Once! You better watch *Easter Parade* this year, young man. I'm serious. I'll be checking up on this."

Tim feels a bit of a buzz coming on, which is odd considering he's only one glass of wine into the evening. Perhaps there's too much pepper on his chicken, he thinks, reaching for his water glass and gulping it down.

"Here's the thing," she goes on, waving a piece of chicken around in the air on the end of her fork for emphasis, "the magic is all in the end scene when Fred Astaire comes to see Judy Garland. He's finally realized that he loves her, but she thinks he loves his old dance partner, and so she's stormed off to her hotel room. He follows her and tells her from the other side of the door that he loves her, and he'll wait all night if need be. And then he knocks on her door— so, so softly—and calls to her, and he says 'Baby... baby,' in a gentle, swoony kind of way, and seriously, it's the most romantic moment on screen, ever. Put that in your *Casablanca* and smoke it."

"And then they end up together?" Tim asks.

"Well, of course, it's not that simple. But I would say that any woman who doesn't fall for Fred Astaire in that instant is a cold, cold woman, indeed. Good heavens, this chicken is to die for."

She breaks off to shout a random, "*woot!*" at the top of her lungs, accompanied by a whistle as the bride and groom kiss at the head table. "Now that's a couple of swells, right there."

She turns back to Tim, takes a slurp of her drink, and leans over again into his personal space. Tim edges over to accommodate her.

"So, tell me, now. What do you think is the most romantic movie of all time?" she says.

"No idea."

"Oh, come on, there must be something. At least three quarters of the movies in the world are about love. Maybe all of them are, if you think about it."

Tim casts about desperately for an answer that will impress her, but put on the spot, he can only come up with one title. "Well... maybe *Star Wars*?" He holds his breath, hoping for the best.

"*Star Wars. STAR WARS.* Did you seriously just say *Star Wars* to me?"

"You know, there's the whole Leia-I-love-you, Han-Solo-I-know moment." He's grasping at straws.

She ponders as she sips her cocktail. Tim marvels that she can, in fact, be silent for at least a few seconds.

"Okay, I'm going to give it to you. *The Empire Strikes Back*, that is, only that one." She waggles a finger in warning.

Tim smiles in relief.

She leans in a little more. "Now tell me…"

It's too much, and Tim, already backed onto the far edge of his seat, slides just a bit too far. His chair wobbles, and he's going down, water glass flying, his head knocking on the chair on the other side of him, arms pinched above him, slumping into an inelegant heap.

"Oh my God! I'm so sorry. So, so sorry!" She reaches over and pulls him back up onto his chair. He holds a hand up to his head, looks down through slightly blurry vision to see that there's a pink blob on the sleeve of his jacket.

"Oh no!" She dips her napkin into her water glass and begins to dab at the spot. "I'm so, so, so sorry."

Tim is dazed, but it seems fitting. He knows the only possible thing to say. "Frankly my dear, I don't give a damn."

She stops dabbing, looks up at him with wide eyes, and her face breaks into a glowing grin. "Now that's romantic." She surveys the damage on his jacket with a frown. "What we need is Club Soda."

Tim nods. "Wait here a minute."

He stands, a little shaky, and manages to elbow his way through chairs and tables of chattering guests. He feels flush, his head is pounding, and he thinks he might be dreaming. He has an idea, skips the bar, and heads over to talk to the DJ. When he returns, he sees he's made a horrible mistake. He's blown everything. She's turned and is talking up the guy on the other side of her, and as he takes his seat, he's left once again facing the centrepiece, nodding dumbly at people walking by. He should know by now that the Grand Gesture only works in the movies.

The song starts, a slow piano rendition with no words. It's barely audible over the hubbub. She'll never hear it. Impossibly, she swivels to him, her mouth falling open, a red-lipsticked, absolutely delighted 'O'.

"Oh. My. God. I cannot believe they are actually playing *Easter Parade* at a wedding. Best. Wedding. Ever." She looks him up and down. "You?" she questions, and he nods as he takes credit, heart rising to his throat. She squeals, "And now we parade—quick, before the speeches start!"

She pulls him to his feet, right there, in the two-foot space between tables. She links her arm in his and leads him forward, and they worm their way through the tables as she waves and hums along with the tune. Tim notes that most of the guests are too busy eating to notice, but maybe this time he wouldn't care if they did.

Eventually, they break free of the tables onto the dance floor in the centre and start a victory lap around the edge.

"I'm Tim," he says as they round a corner.

"Jo."

He smiles; his sister loved *Little Women* growing up, and so he's got the inside track on this one. "Katherine Hepburn or Winona Ryder?"

She gives him a funny look, one eyebrow raised suspiciously, as if he's up to something. "Katherine Hepburn, of course. Did someone tell you already?"

His eyebrows knit together. "Tell me what?"

"Really? No one said anything?"

"No, I swear."

She sighs. "I have three sisters, named Meg, Beth, and Amy."

He whistles. "Seriously!"

"I know. When my parents emigrated, they wanted to give us good English names, and they decided on the *Little Women* theme. I don't think they fully understood what they were doing." She stops walking and turns to look up at him, a little tentative. "What do you think?"

"I think it's kind of magical."

"I think you're kind of magical," she says, reaching up to tap his nose with her finger.

He blushes, and she slips her arm back through his. They resume their promenade. "Does this mean you have a secret real first name?" Tim says.

Jo smiles. "I do, but that's more of a third date kind of revelation."

"Does that mean this is a first date?"

She closes her eyes and rests her head on his shoulder, and they move forward, completing the circle. His head throbs, he smells cherries, and he thinks perhaps Easter is his favourite holiday, after all.

Henry at the Wedding

It's loud in here, too loud for the hearing aid. It creates feedback and turns everything into a dull roar. You remember how it is, Margie, you're the only one I can hear in a crowd. I'd tell you a joke and you'd laugh and I'd hear it, clear as a bell.

It's a wedding this time, Margie. Number eighty-eight: eighty-eight weddings, forty-two funerals, one hundred and seventeen christenings. That's how the life of a pastor adds up. The bride is Katie Brown's daughter—well, she's Katie Hamilton, now. You remember Katie? She used to come to the service every Sunday with that adorable little handbag shaped like a sunflower, so serious and ladylike. Hard to believe she's old enough to have a child, let alone one that's getting married. You used to say I would forget my head if it wasn't screwed on, and I have to admit, I rather have let the library fines stack up, but I remember every bride—and not just because they were pretty young things, so you can keep that thought to yourself. I don't breathe heavy at the ladies these days unless they're one flight up. This one is lovely, though: radiant with youth and smelling like lavender. She stopped by earlier over dinner, making her way around the tables like a good girl. No idea what she was saying—it's loud in here, too loud for the hearing aid—and I saw her eyes start to glaze over and glance around the room as I started to sermonize about sunflower purses and time flying. Still, if she's my last, she's a peach.

You'd certainly be in your element, here, chatting up the strangers at our table or catching up with Bernie and Diane who are up from Florida to see their granddaughter get married. This table is a circle of turned backs and words I can't catch as I smile dumbly at the room, but at least being here proves that I'm still able to be social on occasion. Get out, get a good meal, give off a generally friendly air without seeming too needy. Something different than a dark house, a single cup of tea, and *Mr. Bean's Holiday* for the twentieth time. Growing older is like making pudding: you get lumps if you don't stir.

I hope you noticed that I used your favourite benediction before dinner. You know the one about the flowers? "May your love be the nourishment that causes your soul to bloom and your faith be the light that fills your garden with riches." Come to think of it, I think I said the same one at Katie's wedding. Hopefully she thinks that's a full-circle-thing, rather than a forgetful-old-man-thing. The couple seemed to like it—nice and formal-sounding without being too religious. They didn't want to go too "churchy" with the service. When you were here, I might have made a fuss, but these days I can't seem to get too enthusiastic with my praise. I'm happy to say a few pleasant words in trade for a nice meal and a little champagne. Oh, come on, now, it's only a little sip or two. Even Jesus wouldn't mind too much, I don't think. Maybe if I finish this glass, I'll get up and tell a few jokes. I heard a good one from Lilly the other day when we were doing that computer chatting thing. You'd love it. "What musical instrument is found in the bathroom? A tuba toothpaste!" Ha!

One thing about champagne, you get fewer funny looks when you start chuckling to yourself.

I got to the church a little early today. You know me, I like to be prepared, and truth be told, I find I miss the place these days. That new young fellow has such an odd way of saying words of welcome in his big, booming voice while making me feel completely unwelcome. The smell in there is exactly the same—

old wood and varnish and dusty books—sometimes I think it smells more like home to me than our own house. The garden out back is in full bloom right now. Grown a little wild, I noticed. Sorry about that, but I'm afraid your volunteer force has fallen into a bit of disarray without their fearless leader. Heaven knows, I'm no help. The only thing I grow in a garden is *tired*. Still, it was so pleasant to sit at that sunny back window seat and look out at your beloved begonias and lilies of the valley and feel like the world was evergreen.

That lady who works in the office—Leslie? Or Linda?—came out when she saw me and explained, very loudly and very slowly, that they didn't have the plant sale this year without you to run it. I think she meant to be kind, but she does annoy me with the way she thinks I've turned into a simpleton without you to look after me... to look after everything. I suppose it isn't that far from the truth, although I keep forgetting to tell you, in case you are worried, Margie, that I have been using the grocery list you left me faithfully once a week. I hope you don't mind, but I added a few frozen dinners to the list, a rite of passage marking me as a true hermit. What's with all the mushrooms, by the way? I haven't the foggiest idea of what to do with them. Did we really eat mushrooms every week? Maybe this is your idea of one last joke? In any case, I keep buying them because they're on the list, and they're providing a nice, rich compost for your rosebushes, which are thriving. I guess your knack for making things grow *lives on*. See what I did there? Ha! I always get in Shirley's line at the cash, as she always asks after you. I don't have the heart to tell her the truth, so I say you're doing, "About the same, about the same." It's one moment a week when I'm not *just* me, but part of "we" again. I like it.

I can't seem to convince Sarah that I'm doing just fine, though, and she has been worrying at me to move up to her place. I know it's only a few hours' drive, but I could never bring myself to leave your gardens behind. Did I tell you that Frank has gone to live with his daughter on the west coast? And that I said a few words at Beatrice Shilling's memorial last month? I took the last few of your tulips with me. These days, the phone never rings with good news, I'm afraid. You had the right idea, going early. When being run out of town, get out in front and make it look like a parade, am I right? Still, it would be nice to see Lilly each day. Her little voice has that same quality yours had, cuts right through the babble, clear as a bell. I have a good joke for her: "What did the flower say to the bee? Buzz off!" I think she'll like it.

It's almost time for the dancing to start. They're testing the sound system and that's making it loud in here, too loud for the hearing aid. Living alone, you get used to the quiet. I know if you were here you'd be fixing to get out on the floor cutting a rug, but I think I'll wait until I can get a slice of cake and then head home. The older you get, the more the tripping becomes less light and more fantastic. I know you're smiling at that one. Oh, this song! You remember this one, don't you, Margie? *God Only Knows What I'd Be Without You.* Huh. Kind of wish the big guy had kept that tidbit to himself.

The nice thing about champagne is, you get fewer funny looks when your eyes tear up.

There's some kind of draw going on now, and everyone is looking under their side plates. I have a purple dot on mine. Oh, I see, I have won the centrepiece. Well, what a lovely thing it is, too: pink carnations and a spray of something small and purple. Smells pretty. Katie is looking at me funny; I think she expects me to give it to her, wants to press them into a book maybe, or wonders what an old man like myself is going to do with flowers. But I know what I will do with them. It's late, but it's never too late to stop by the cemetery on my way home and lie there with my head on the ground next to yours, together under the light of a thousand stars. You'll love them, Margie, you really will. God willing, I'll see you soon.

Claire at the Wedding

There's a whole closet full of dresses—dresses from happy times and far away places—but nothing is working. She's lost too much weight, Claire thinks, and nothing goes with a head scarf, but she's determined to find something. Étienne didn't even show her the invitation when it arrived. It was for one of his team members at work, not worth the trouble, he'd said. But she'd fished it out of the garbage and insisted they go. Claire loves a wedding. They're all about hope, and lately, her life has been so restricted to the narrow present that it'll be nice to think about the future for a change, even if it's just one day, even if it's stolen from someone else.

It's been a month, or perhaps a lifetime, since Dr. Chambers broke the news that they hadn't gotten into the experimental treatment study they were hoping for. They were only taking women over thirty-five, and Claire was still too young. Since then, the good doctor has been saying less and less at each appointment, asking a lot of questions without offering many answers. Last week he asked to speak to Étienne alone. Claire knows why; he isn't to mention the words palliative care in her presence, and she supposes, in good conscience, he feels the need to bring it up with some member of her team. Étienne had said nothing to her, though. She feels such a surge of appreciation, such a surge of love every time she thinks of this little kindness, this little marker that shows how he knows her, understands what she needs right now and always.

Claire pulls out a sundress with purple flowers, frowns, puts it back. She's given up on the falsies and bra but those spaghetti straps just won't fly; the tattoos from her treatment will be visible and will make everyone uncomfortable, older ladies looking on with pity, younger women staring in hopes of finding some difference between them that will act like a talisman of protection. She tries another: black with white dots, a higher neckline with little cap sleeves. Will it be alright to wear black? She supposes it will have to do.

Étienne slips his hands around her waist, nuzzles into her neck. She's grateful he's never shown one bit of hesitancy when touching her, never once made her feel less than.

"Did you sleep okay?" he asks, and she says yes, although it was another night full of psychedelic dreams, spinning images filling her brain from the drugs or the new tumours in her head, or both. She'd dreamt last night again about the train—the same one she feels compelled to sketch every day, especially now that she isn't working and even reading is becoming too tiring. It's an old steam train, like a mix of the Hogwarts Express and Thomas the Tank Engine, cheerful somehow, its puffs of steam seeming to whisper, "come along, come along" with every exhale. She sometimes waits for the train at the station, sometimes boards and takes a spot by the window, feels the soft suede of the dark green seats. Then the train inevitably twists and turns into fireworks or unicorns dancing on rainbows or exploding constellations, and she wakes up.

Forget the head scarf, she thinks. It's too warm, and she doesn't want anything to choke out the summer sun. She'll go with The Full Wispy—let 'em stare.

ॐ

Claire sits on a bench behind the church, drinking in the heady perfume of the garden which is bursting with blooms. Someone has put a lot of love into it. She didn't quite make it through the ceremony—it was too hot in there, and she got dizzy, but the garden has the feel of a holy place, too, and she still feels tethered to the ritual, like she's a part of things. She hears a small shuffling behind her and turns to see Étienne peeking out of the door; now that he's been spotted he smiles to hide his concern. She pats the seat next to her, and he comes to join her, taking her hand in his as they sit silently, enjoying the warm summer day. She wishes she had a picture of this garden. Maybe she'll get out her watercolours and try to recreate it from memory some day, on a good day. Maybe she'll add it to her portfolio, finally pull together that coffee table book of her work she's been thinking about self-publishing.

She can't help stealing glances at him, her lovely husband, his glasses slightly thicker than hers, his sandy hair almost the same shade as her own but looking uncombed as always, his deep blue eyes that light up when he smiles. They're a matched set, she and him, salt and pepper shakers. She knew it the day she met him while on exchange in France. She'd caught a whiff of his scent, exactly like freshly baked bread in her grandmother's kitchen, the familiar smell taking her breath away in such a foreign place. Later, it was confirmed by the way her head was just the right height to lay on his shoulder, the way they both loved mayonnaise on their French fries, the way they both liked to spend Sunday mornings nestled in bed with strong coffee and a book of poetry. They were married before the year was out. When she returned home with a French husband, her mother chuckled at her impulsivity and confidence—"Same old Claire"—and her parents welcomed him as one of their own. He fit in with her two brothers like he'd always been a member of the family. "Part of the crew," said her father, and to Claire, it felt like a hole had been filled.

Étienne leans over to her. "If you're not feeling up to the reception, we can absolutely skip it."

She shakes her head. "No way! I have lipstick on. Lipstick! We are going out to a party, my friend, whether you like it or not."

He smiles. "How about we go home and lie down for a bit first?"

She nods. "Sure thing, if you feel like you need a rest. I get it, old man."

He slips his arm around her waist and helps her to her feet. They walk together, arms wrapped around each other, to the car, heading for home and tea and blankets and comfort.

❧

At dinner, Claire isn't able to eat much, but she does her best to try a bite or two of everything, feeling more than tasting the rich buttery smoothness of the chicken, catching a whiff of the orange peels that top the sugary chocolate cake before they turn metallic on her tongue. *Smells like Christmas,* she thinks. She's fading a little, despite a glorious nap in the afternoon, curled up in the bed next to Étienne, his book pages making a little lullaby for her. *What are you reading,* she'd said, then drifted off before hearing the answer, finding her first deep, dreamless sleep in weeks.

It had been enough to help her feel almost like her old self at the reception, almost fully alive. She's met Étienne's co-workers before, the people at their table: hilarious Carl and his giggly wife Samantha who are both on the team, and gentlemanly Rohan who, it turns out, has the most charming wife whose name Claire can't remember. The group is lively and the conversation breezy. God, how freeing it feels to just talk—to talk about movies and books and politics with kind acquaintances, to feel the buzz of being in a room full of people, squealing children, and perky bridesmaids and to absorb an underlying hum of pure energy. It's worth the fight against the ache in her bones to be a part of it.

The sun has gone down. She can tell because her left eye is starting to do that blurry thing, the faint warning signs of a headache echo in the back of her head. But she's determined to have her first dance. Her last dance. Her last first dance.

When she's had enough of pushing cake bites around her plate, she gives Étienne a little jerk of her head towards the dance floor, raising her eyebrows. He grimly takes her hand—he's never been much of a dancer—and walks her out slowly. She's in flats, for balance, so he's almost a full head taller than her, but she can still find that sweet spot on his shoulder where her head fits perfectly. He wraps his arms around her, and she thinks that if they were made of rubber, they'd probably be able to wind around her a few times. They sway gently to the music, a song Claire remembers from grade school dances, something about a runaway train.

Étienne leans down to kiss the top of her head, and Claire responds by stepping on his foot.

"Sorry!" She winces.

He says with a chuckle, "It will be alright, my foot will live."

Claire stops moving and looks up at him. "No, I mean sorry. Sorry for it all. Sorry for everything."

Étienne looks confused.

Claire sighs. "This must feel like one huge flimflam to you."

"Flin...?"

"Like... one big swindle. A rip off. Everything gone wrong. Nothing as advertised. You marry some foreign chick, you cross an ocean just to be with her, and it turns out, it's not even going to work out."

Étienne smiles sadly. "You will never be a flinflon, Claire." He spins her out with uncharacteristic dramatic flair, twirls her back in close, their noses almost touching, and they sway again.

"I want you to move back to France," says Claire. "Afterwards."

He sighs. "I do not wish to talk to about this."

"I've been thinking, and it makes the most sense. You should go home, find your home again."

Étienne frowns. "But here is home, too. Your home is my home." He stops swaying. "You will be here. Wherever you go, I go, remember?"

She takes one hand and places it over his heart. "Wherever you are, I'll be there."

He shakes his head. "My life is here now."

"It's here now. But it won't be in a few months. Go home, go back to France, and this can all stay a beautiful, passing dream you once had."

Étienne smiles. "You are already a beautiful dream, Claire. Also, I do not want to move back in with my parents."

He gives an exaggerated shudder and she smiles, too.

"Okay, you can get your own place. But France is where you belong."

"I belong here, too. I'd miss Thanksgiving at your parents' house, when everyone eats until bursting. If I keep going there for the next twenty years I may actually come to understand football."

"But don't you miss that café on Rue Dupuis where you proposed, and then spilled your coffee everywhere when I said yes?"

He chuckles. "I thought you did the proposing."

She elbows him. "Well, I guess it was kind of a mutual thing."

"The library here is our library. Nowhere else in the world is going to have a giant statue of a pigeon out front. Where else will I be able to tell my pigeon joke?"

"I've heard it. It's not funny."

He sniffs. "Some people think it's funny."

"No one thinks it's funny," she teases.

He tries again. "There is the market downtown. Your face lights up there. You want to try everything, taste everything. Remember when we bought one of every fruit we could find, then sat by the river and cut into each one? That was a good day."

"Are you saying there are no picnics in France? Home of baguettes and cheese? Home of luncheons on the Champ de Mars? I'll get you a nice Renoir picture book next time we're at the library."

He smiles but shakes his head at the same time.

"Just tell me you'll think about it," she says.

"I will think about it, Claire, but this is not your decision. Let us just dance, yes?"

She closes her eyes and folds into his chest once again. Étienne smells like old books and arrowroot cookies and freshly baked bread, nothing antiseptic, nothing medical. He is as real as she is ethereal, as solid as she is shadowy. He is a tether to this world for the two of them, two of a kind, salt and pepper shakers.

"Wherever I am, there you will be," he whispers, as much to himself as to her, it seems.

She could swear she hears a train whistle, far off in the distance, calling her to come along, come along, come along home.

Luke at the Wedding

"Y ou can't be a writer if you haven't truly lived," Luke says. "So, when I was nineteen I said screw it. My dad was pushing medical school, a nice safe option, but I needed to get out! See the world! So, I went to New York, and my second day there—I'd slept in the bus terminal the first night, one eye open for the cops of course—that's when I met him. J.D. Salinger himself, next in line to me at the deli. Jerry, as I came to call him, getting himself a ham on rye."

He sits back to let his audience drink this in, their eyes starry, leaning forward to catch every word. It still works, the Salinger bit, despite the mystique of the man fading into history more and more each year. This time, it's for the benefit of a circle of cousins and friends about Iris' age, his wife earning him a spot at the young people's table. God, he loves the young:

not yet jaded enough to realize, that for all his preaching about adventure, he's done nothing but teach the same tired courses at the same middling university for the past twenty years. They look up at him with adoring eyes, worship that he's almost, but not quite, tired of receiving.

Iris had been the same—another bright-eyed co-ed with her dark hair in a librarian bun, olive skin glowing behind delicately framed glasses as she sat in the front row of his Lit 101 class, eating up his tall tales of life as Jerry's sometime assistant, sometime wingman. He'd barely noticed her as his mouth moved on autopilot, trotting out the New York Stories for that year's freshmen, hitting the punchlines effortlessly with familiar phrases he knew played well, while his mind wandered to thoughts of dinner and sex and whether or not his jeans made him look over-the-hill. She'd turned out to be different, though; their after class "study sessions" in his office had somehow expanded into sleepovers, brunches, dinner dates. He'd since come to realize that Iris had a quiet but firm way of ignoring everything anyone said and merrily doing whatever the hell she wanted anyway. Despite his protests and contentment with the usual flow of a school year— the girl dazzled, then bored, then tired, then gone—

he'd found himself hosting dinner parties with a bona fide girlfriend.

When he'd told Paula he was getting married again, she'd laughed, not out of bitterness but surprise, and apologised immediately. But Luke knew what she was picturing: wedding photos where their son, Tyler, as Best Man, looked more like the groom, with Luke as some poorly placed father of the bride, or perhaps an exalted favourite uncle. He imagined the guests smiling grimly at him to his face, gossiping behind his back about May-December romances.

In the end, it had been fine. Lovely, actually—different and unique. Iris was a radiant, barefoot bride, and he'd been delighted to give her the day she'd wanted: a simple backyard event full of flowers and sunshine and the illusion, he thought, of a long, happy future. Afterwards, he'd sometimes wake before her and be amazed at her beauty as she slept next to him, so pure and peaceful and yes, dammit, so young. He'd lie there and wonder if this really was his life, or was it a dream, a fragile bubble that would pop the minute she opened her eyes—or perhaps the minute she heard him tell the Salinger story again.

Iris lays a gentle hand on his arm, the other cradling her swollen belly. "Dear? The baby and I would love a club soda," she says in his ear, a simple request that suddenly seems so intimate to him, his throat seizes up.

"Of course, sweetheart."

Luke rises and is a few steps away from the table before he thinks to wonder if this is just an errand or if he's been dismissed. He looks back to see the gaggle of cousins leaning into Iris, eager for news of the baby. Iris has taken his place in the spotlight.

At the bar, there's a young guy with red hair and freckles working the pumps, looking barely old enough to drink himself. "What'll it be?" he says.

"A club soda with a twist of lime and... A bourbon with ice." He pauses. What the hell, it's a special occasion. "Make it a double."

The bartender pulls out the glass and ice with polished flair, sliding the drink over like they're in an old-time saloon. Luke savours his first sip. It burns a little. The bride and groom tried to save money on the open bar by avoiding the really good stuff, he thinks, but as soon as the warmth hits his stomach he decides, magnanimously, to forgive them.

"My partner just went to get more limes," says the kid behind the bar. "Want to take the club soda as is or wait?"

Luke's in no rush to return to the table. "I'll wait," he says, leaning on the rich cherry wood like a cattleman in from a long ride.

The bartender tries to busy himself behind the bar, but he's clearly running out of things to do as the guests find their seats for dinner, and the area clears. Soon, the silence becomes awkward.

"Great wedding," Luke offers.

"I know, right?" The bartender smiles agreeably.

Luke leans in. "You must have seen your fair share of these things, bride after bride after bride, eh? Tell me, is this one any different?"

"Oh, you bet; it's really special," says the kid, disappointing Luke, who was hoping for more than just a cheap grab at a good tip. "You can really see how much they're in love."

Luke leans back for a good look at the boy. He's gangly and awkward and young—young enough to be eager to please, sure, but old enough, Luke thinks, that he should be doing something greater with his life than serving cheap alcohol at cookie-cutter weddings. This evening isn't going to give Luke anything new to write about, nothing has, nothing for years. But it's not too late for this kid, he just needs get some great experiences under his belt.

Luke reaches across the bar, offering his hand. "Luke."

"Matt."

Luke nods as they shake. "Great to meet you. So, what do you do, Matt?"

Matt looks a little confused. "Uh, I serve drinks?"

Luke chuckles—kids these days. "No, I mean when you're not serving drinks. What feeds your soul? What's at the heart of you?"

Matt looks a little uncomfortable, but that's the goal here. "Well, I have my music."

Luke smacks the bar—a little too hard. He's downing his drink too quickly, but he's thinking it might not be a good idea to show up at the table with it in hand. "That's fantastic! Music! What are you working on?"

"Well, nothing concrete, so far, but me and a couple of guys are talking about forming a band. I have a few songs ready." He blushes as if saying it out loud makes it dirty.

"No, no, that's wonderful! You've got to get that band together, get the show on the road. Now is the time, Matt! These are the days when you need to be out there, meeting people, seeing new places, doing a lot of drugs..." He laughs at Matt's wide eyes. "You're young. You can handle it."

Matt gives an uncertain tip of his head. "I guess."

Luke feels the story rising up. He can't stop it; it's second nature to him. "Why, when I was your age, I ran off to New York City, all on my own. Worked for a summer for J.D. Salinger. Met him in line at a sandwich shop while he ordered a ham on rye."

"No kidding! We had to read *Catcher in the Rye* twice in high school."

Luke tips his bourbon at Matt. "Called him Jerry, even."

Matt looks suitably impressed, and Luke feels the bourbon—he thinks it's the bourbon—making that familiar warm feeling in his gut.

"Yeah, I ended up working for the guy, something like an assistant, or a paid friend—not in that way!—just hanging out, you know? He'd send me on these wild errands—twenty blocks north for a specific colour of ink—and tell me not to come back until I'd met five new people." Luke could tell his voice was getting louder, warmed by the subject and the drink. "Then we'd sit up all night, smoking and drinking, and I'd tell him about the street, the crowds, the characters, and by morning we'd write and write and order in egg sandwiches. It was brilliant." He paused for well-practiced effect.

Matt looks thoughtful. "Man, this stuff is great. It would make a great song."

"A great... what?" *That isn't what they usually say,* Luke thinks.

"Yeah, a great tune! I use a lot of stuff people tell me to make songs. People tell you all kinds of crazy stories when you're a bartender. Really, you don't have to get out there to find life—life kinda comes to you."

Luke feels fuzzy around the edges. He downs the last of his drink and notices his hand shake just once, just a hair, as he puts the glass carefully, precisely, back on the bar.

Matt is humming. "New York in the summertime... new in town, didn't have a dime... Hey, that works. Mind if I jot it down?" He pulls a notebook and pencil from somewhere below, takes a step back and perches the book on his knee. "Met the catcher in the rye in a sandwich shop... he said grab hold of life and never let it drop..."

"Wait... that's not it..." Luke feels himself spluttering, watching from outside, wondering what's happening.

The other bartender has returned, a small woman with close-cropped pink hair. Matt murmurs at her and soon an iced glass of club soda, with its lime in place, is full and waiting.

"Anything else, sir?" asks Pink Hair while Matt continues to scribble away in the background. Luke recognises it, a memory stirring from long ago; the creative muse has come to visit, but not in his corner.

Luke would like another bourbon. Yes, he would. But he can feel a blurry kind of anger gnawing at the fringes of his vision, and he knows he's already had more than he should. He shakes his head and grabs the soda, spilling a bit on the bar, something for Matt to clean up, he hopes, maybe enough to drown out the creative spark. How could he be so complacent, so careless? He's given it all away, now; he's given everything away. Soon, his best story will look like a rehash of some *American Top 40* pop hit, a cliché that teenagers sing at full volume on prom night, fists hammering the air as they rock out. He may as well stand up there in his next Lit 101 class and recite the lyrics to Bon Jovi's *Livin' On a Prayer*, for all the authenticity it will appear to have.

He turns to head back to the table. He can hear Matt calling after him—something about "ink" making a great rhyme for "drink"—but he's heard enough. He looks around wildly. Wasn't the table to the left? No, there, to the right. He can see Iris' head bobbing gently in soft conversation. He stumbles to his place next to her and sloshes the drink a little as he sets it down too heavily on the table.

Iris looks up. "Everything okay?"

Luke doesn't quite know how to answer that. "Sure, honey, sure."

Iris smiles, a knowing smile he's come to recognize as indulgence—a kindness he never feels he deserves. She leans over to whisper in his ear, only flinching a bit, barely noticeable, when she smells the alcohol on his breath. "You gonna save a dance for me tonight?" she flirts. He nods distractedly.

Suddenly everyone at their table is up, chairs scraping. Something about a *Cha Cha Slide* and getting the bride and groom to kiss. They bubble over to the dance floor in their exhausting way, making their own clique.

"Why don't you go with them," he says, hoping the self-pity in his voice is masked.

"No, I'm happy here," she says, laying her head gently on his shoulder, sinking into his side.

Luke pulls back so he can look her full in the face. "What do you see in an old guy like me, anyway?" he asks, a question he's had on his lips for months, years even, but never dared to ask.

Iris laughs, a lovely twinkle in her eye, and meets his gaze. She lifts her fingers in two L-shapes, creating a frame around his face like she's looking through a camera, and squints. "I see a man who is passionate, who is creative, and who is loving. I see a man who has been waiting to do something great, and it's been a long time, and you're starting to not believe, but it's in there. I saw it that first day in class. You have something gleaming in your eyes, like an idea waiting to be born. Some day it'll ripen and burst out, and then you're going to surprise yourself with how amazing you can be."

She pauses and leans over to kiss him on the cheek. "And if he's ready to embrace it, I see a man who is ready for another adventure in fatherhood. Think of what a great story that will be!"

Luke gives her a wry smile. He's been thinking that he's too old for new adventures, but maybe this ride isn't over yet. Maybe now is the time to let life come to him for a change. Hell, it's already here, isn't it? There is still life to be lived, right?

Maybe her faith will be enough for both of them.

"You bet I'll save you a dance," he says, reaching out to touch the life inside her and feeling a flutter.

Juliet at the Wedding

uliet fingers the note in her palm, smiling in anticipation. She likes to poke her finger with the hard corners. This is no small scrap with a few words jotted down, no shopping list, but a full sheet of white bond with cramped writing on both sides, folded so many times it's like a block of wood in her hand. It feels almost warm to her touch, the words that are captured in the letter have a life to them that can be sensed.

Juliet has a secret, and secrets were never made to be kept.

∎

Juliet reapplies her lipstick in the mirror—even in this harsh bathroom lighting, it's a flattering shade.

The new dress she has for the occasion isn't hurting, either: red satin with a sweetheart neckline and slight empire waist. She stands out like a bloody slash in the background of the snapshots of the other guests. What's that saying? Looking good is the best revenge? Mission accomplished.

There's a giggling bridesmaid at the next sink over, chatting it up with a friend. They're talking about him; he was her partner as they walked down the aisle, two by two, faking romance. She thinks he's cute, wonders if he's single. Juliet wonders if she should say something.

She imagines:

"Oh no, honey, you don't want any piece of that action. He's a liar and a cheat, a lying cheat, and no good to any woman. He's pretty on the outside but ugly on the inside, if you get what I'm saying."

She smiles to herself, but she can't bring herself to say the words out loud—such a silly girl would only think she's bitter and jaded, anyway. She'd never understand.

Juliet notices a dead fly on the edge of the sink. It's iridescent body gleams under the fluorescents. *How beautiful*, she thinks.

Now is the time. The wedding party is busy welcoming people at the door in a receiving line. There he is, flirting with the old ladies, holding the hands of the younger ones a little too long. She's standing at the head table, ready to slip the note under his dinner plate, if she can only figure out which spot is his. She keeps losing count, distracted by the scene at the entrance.

God, it must be nice to live in a world where everyone loves you. Where you always get what you want, where everything is easy. She'd said as much to him, the last time she slept at his place. They'd fought in the morning, over coffee, after she found the text messages. She'd tried to stay calm, but the way he brushed it off as nothing was infuriating. "You're so black and white," he'd said; she'd thrown her mug at his head and walked out.

That was before she knew the whole of it, of course. If she'd known then what she knew now, maybe she'd have thrown the whole pot. Now, he'd see how black and white the world could be, how a pink line on a stick could change everything.

She can't wait to see the look on his face when he finds her note. What a show it'll be! His face falling, mouth hanging open, the stupid loopy grin he always wears finally wiped clean away. He'll look for her in the crowd, and there she'll sit, triumphant. Then what? She hasn't thought that far ahead. She supposes they'll have to meet. Maybe he'll ask her to talk, a look of desperation on his face; maybe lawyers will have to be involved. Whatever happens, happens, she thinks. In any case, she'll have the upper hand; she'll be the one holding all the cards. She had a dream once, and this might be a twisted version of it, but she's going to make it happen, he'll see, he'll see. He's going to find out what it means to be *accountable*.

Based on his position in the receiving line next to the best man, his spot is third from the end... no, fourth. Third? Juliet taps her foot in frustration, just as something grabs at her ankle. A hand. A little brown hand, and behind it, a pair of enormous brown eyes. It's the flower girl—what is her name? Juliet remembers from the program: Ella. She's under the table, the white cloth floating around her like a blanket fort.

"Come in!" she says.

Juliet looks around, left and right. Yes, the girl definitely means to address her. Juliet crouches down, awkward in her short red dress, teetering momentarily on her high heels.

"Hello?"

"Come in, come in!" Ella waves her hands urgently.

Juliet frowns. "Um... I'm kinda busy right now."

"But she'll see you! Hide!"

Ella grabs Juliet's hand and pulls, hard, almost dislodging the letter in her palm. Juliet loses her balance, landing harder than she'd like on her bottom. She makes a token effort to pull the tablecloth over her head, hoping her hair isn't getting messed up. She gives her hip a rueful rub. "Who are we hiding from?"

Ella giggles, then leans into Juliet like a co-conspirator. "My mom! Shh... She'll never find us."

Juliet leans back, has a long look at the girl. What is she, three? Four? How old are kids when they learn to talk? Juliet looks at Ella like an explorer stumbling across a wild animal in the jungle, wary, watchful, curious.

Ella peeks under the far side of the tablecloth. "I see her!" she squeals. She scrambles backwards, bumping into Juliet, squirming into her side as if Juliet is good camouflage. Juliet's hand closes over the note, keeping it safe, but her other arm reaches instinctively around Ella.

"I like your dress," says Ella, curling up to Juliet. "It's soft, and red is my second favourite colour. I had a red dress when I was little, but now I am bigger, and it is too small, and I cried when my mom said I had to give it away, so my mom says I can keep it for now, and maybe we will get a doll that will fit it."

Juliet smiles, charmed in spite of herself. "I like your dress too—pink is my second favourite colour."

Ella grins. "Did you see the flowers? Down here around the bottom? There's one here and here and over here. There are three in one big bunch, and that is the best part, you can feel them if you want, they are bumpy, but it is nice. Do you know thumb war?"

Juliet raises her eyebrows; the turn is a sharp one. "Uh... no? Want to show me?" She's sweet, Juliet thinks, but maybe if they make a little more noise thumb warring, they'll be found, and Ella will move on. The plan is going off track—she's forgotten for a moment what she was supposed to be doing. She has to open her hand to make sure the note is still there.

"It goes like this. You hold my hand, like this, no you need your thumb out. Then we touch thumbs a bunch of times, like this, and we say, one two three four, I declare a thumb war."

Ella pauses expectantly.

"You have to say it now."

Juliet grimaces, unsure. "Ah... one two, three four..."

"I declare a thumb war," Ella finishes impatiently. "Okay, then we try to pin the other guy's thumb down, like this, but you have to be nice because my thumb is little, and Miss Hamilton gets mad when the big kids always win."

She starts to tussle at Juliet's hand, and Juliet puts up some token resistance until Ella pins her thumb down. Ella frowns. "No, that was too easy. Do it again."

The struggle is repeated, but Juliet thinks to herself that nothing is ever easy, not thumb wars, not pregnancy tests, not sitting on the ground under the head table at a wedding, hiding from mothers and broken hearts and life. There are only hard choices and disappointments and always getting the short end of the stick.

Not this time, she thinks, not this time.

"Gotcha!" Juliet yelps as she pins Ella's thumb, and Ella pouts and pulls her hand away.

"That was too hard," she whines.

Juliet looks at her kindly, softly. She can see a whole future for this girl, a whole life of things being hard. "You sound like Goldilocks—too easy, too hard," she teases, trying to coax out a smile.

Ella grumbles but relents. "Baby bear is my favourite," she says.

"Do you have a bear at home?"

Ella's eyes widen. "I have three bears!"

"Wow. That's pretty awesome."

"Want to come over and see them later?"

Juliet finds, to her surprise, that maybe she does and discovers she is nodding. Ella takes her hand and leans into Juliet's side. They sit in silence for a moment. Ella's hand in Juliet's is sticky and warm and comforting. Easy.

Just then, the curtain is pulled back.

"Ella, what are you doing down here?" says a tall woman with dirty-blonde hair pulled into a ponytail. There's a tired, tender tone in her voice that can only come with motherhood, maybe amplified due to her youth.

She seems so young, too young, younger than me, Juliet thinks.

"Come on now, get out, it's time to get ready for the big entrance thing."

Ella squeals again, crawling out and jumping into her mother's arms. The woman gives Juliet a wry smile of apology and a whispered thanks for the time spent with her daughter. She nods at Juliet in a strange way—a way Juliet isn't used to at all—as if they are peers, caregivers with a child in common. Mother to mother, perhaps.

The woman scoops Ella up, and they turn away, Ella babbling on, their heads close together. Juliet watches them go, and for a moment sees herself in those shoes, in that role, a little head bowed to her own. She swallows hard, blots at one eye with a finger, worrying about her mascara running. She shakes her head, then realizes she's going to have to figure out how to stand up in her little dress and her ridiculous heels. Maybe it wouldn't be so bad to just hide there a little longer, to feel safe, to feel peace. Make the world a little smaller for just a moment or two.

Can it be that simple? A table fort and a pretty pink dress and thumb wars? Maybe she's the one who has been making everything hard. She pulls up the tablecloth a little to peek out—the wedding party is still over there, and he's still glad-handing the guests. *Smile on, fool*, she thinks. *You don't know what you're missing. You don't know what you're going to be missing.*

She has been seeking punishment, but she realizes that maybe what she'd be offering him is a reward. A chance for a prize, a special kind of joy. Something she should be hoarding, not giving away.

What I need, Juliet thinks, *Is a new way of winning.*

Maybe, she'll be able to figure it all out. Maybe, a different kind of twosome—a parent, a child—will be where she belongs. Maybe, they'll be okay; maybe, they'll be happy; maybe, they'll even be—Juliet dares to dream—easy.

Maybe, some secrets were meant to be kept, after all.

Kate at the Wedding

ate looks at her watch, a small pearl-faced oval on a delicate gold chain. A gift from her parents on her graduation from middle school. It still fits her wrist after all these years, and it's almost embarrassing how much she's been looking forward to wearing it tonight. There's not much call for formal wear, these days, so it hardly ever sees the light of day outside her jewelry box. She's even selected her outfit to match: a champagne pantsuit with a sprinkle of sequins around the edge of the tunic top, perfect for the mother of the bride.

They're running on time, mostly, about fifteen minutes or so behind the master schedule. Page one of the big binder—the *Wedding Bible* as Bruce likes to call it. Kate doesn't have much of a sense of humour when it comes to the binder, and Bruce often earns himself a big old Bruce Eyeroll for his gentle mockery. It's a big event, and she and her daughter have been working for weeks to make everything perfect. One whole day of dreamy perfection. The reality of muted houses and empty nests can wait until the morning after; she'll have the rest of her life to figure that part out.

So far, it all seems to be going according to plan. Mostly.

"The carnations were supposed to be pink," Kate frets, eyeing the table's centrepiece.

Bruce reaches over and pats her arm. "Just let it go, honey."

"These are clearly salmon," says Kate. "Don't you think they're more salmon than pink?"

"I think they look lovely." Bruce lifts his eyebrows and nods, his face offering the look that Kate knows means *relax, it's okay, everything is going to be okay.*

Kate huffs. "I suppose it's too late, now. But still, I'm going to call the florist on Monday and give them a piece of my mind."

Bruce shrugs at this, his annoying way of indicating he knows Kate will never do it, and she sighs, knowing the truth of her own lack of resolve.

"At least the cake arrived in one piece and looks right. I was so sure they were going to mess up that lacy bit around the top layer. The woman at the store didn't seem to understand a thing I was saying to her."

Bruce slides her an impish grin. "Well, we haven't cut into it yet..."

Kate laughs and dishes out a little punch to his arm. "You're playing with fire, there, buddy."

"Well, I'm a guy who lives on the edge," Bruce says in his favourite James Bond voice. He turns to his food. "Try the chicken, dear, it's actually pretty good."

"I can't eat a thing; I'm too jittery."

"But the hard part is over! This is the fun part! I hope you have your dancing shoes on."

He shimmies his shoulders and bites his lip in an imitation of Bad Dad Dancing, and Kate chuckles in spite of herself. She doesn't bother to point out that her feet are killing her; it's been ages since she wore heels, but she can always kick them off like one of the bridesmaids. It's practically tradition to dance barefoot at a wedding; she did it at her own almost thirty years ago. She stiffens at a few familiar notes coming from the DJ table. "Is that... *Easter Parade* they're playing?"

Bruce talks around the bite of potato in his mouth. "Oh, pish, no one cares. Look around! Everyone is having a great time."

Kate does look, but there's only one person who she truly cares about right now: her lovely daughter, radiant at the head table. She's laughing over her glass of champagne, and Kate catches her giving the groom a little wink. A blue lace handkerchief is worked into her bouquet. It's her something old, blue and borrowed; four generations in Kate's family have carried it at their own weddings. Kate had shown up with a fake ruby ring from a bubblegum machine last week—*for your something new*, Kate had said, and they'd both had a good giggle. Kate's pleased to see the gaudy thing catching the light every so often on her daughter's right hand, like an in-joke for just the two of them.

Kate's going to miss her. The awareness that soon—tomorrow—the house will have a deeper level of quiet has been hovering on the edges of her mind, and now it's pushing its way forward. Being a parent sometimes feels like one long, drawn-out goodbye. A farewell of inches, a little more each day, so you hardly notice. Your little one is up there in a white dress and pearls, smiling at her new husband, when just one moment ago you were standing on the porch step waving goodbye as she headed out to her first day of kindergarten. Suddenly, it's the last day your home is also her home, and it's a mystery how you got to this place.

Her daughter's room at their house is empty, the dresser drawers hollow, the bedside lamp already moved to the new apartment. She's their baby; the last one to go. After today, she and Bruce will go home to a house that's a little bit quieter, a little bit emptier, and become a family of two again. Kate shakes her head; thoughts like this aren't helping. She promised herself she'd treat today as a positive thing, one last gift for her daughter, a perfect day to start things off right. She never could stand old biddies who cry at weddings.

Kate catches her daughter's eye and gives her a smile. *Almost there, honey. It's all going so well. I'm proud of you.*

Isn't it odd, Kate thinks, how mothers need their daughters as much as the other way around. But there's time to worry about that tomorrow. She checks her gold watch again and wonders if she should prompt the caterer to bring out dessert. Sometimes she has to take care of everything.

❧

Kate is about to make another run to the bar to make sure they're well stocked for the dancing, maybe check in with the kitchen to remind them about the special little cooler she's brought for the

top cake layer, to be saved for a future christening—
rushing things, she knows, but she can't help it—
when the M.C. stands up to introduce Bruce. He gives
Kate's hand a squeeze, rises to a smattering of
applause, and bounds up to the podium. Kate is
grateful she hasn't been pressured to speak, too.
Bruce is the ambassador for their family; he's easy
with people and tells a good story around the dinner
table while Kate tidies up in the background.

Kate realizes she has no idea what Bruce is going
to say. She's been too busy with appointments and
fittings, a blur of credit card bills, to even ask for a
preview. *Everything will be fine,* she assures herself.
*Everyone loves Bruce, he's going to be great, and the bar
is fine, and the cake is fine, and no one even notices the
centrepieces.*

Other than me. But that's it. Probably.

"I've been asked to say a few words about
marriage," says Bruce into the mic. "When I got
married, I remember my lovely wife, Kate, wanted
everything to be perfect. 'A wonderful start to a
wonderful life,' she said. Well, if you were there—
and I know some of you were—you know things
didn't start out so well.

"It rained. Of course, it rained. A torrential
downpour. On the way to the reception, my brother
braked hard to avoid hitting a squirrel in the road,

and the cake slid forward off the back seat and landed in a heap on the floor of the car. The guests arriving at the reception got quite an eyeful—he and my mother scraping up the cake one spoonful at a time, bent over the back seat in their fancy clothes, their backsides sticking out in the pouring rain. I think, at one point, their plan was to have everyone grab a fork and line up in the parking lot to get themselves a scoop."

Kate winces; she can still remember how furious she was, how important it seemed at the time that the cake was ruined, that everything was ruined. This time through the story, though, everyone laughs, and she feels her mouth turning up into a small smile— maybe it's the champagne.

"And our photographer has become a bit of a legend—standing right in front of us during the ceremony. We should have asked the guests if they were there for the bride, groom, or photographer. I never thought our first kiss as man and wife would be set to the soundtrack of a camera shutter three inches from my head."

Bruce gives her an intimate little wink. She remembers how they laughed in the honeymoon suite, Bruce doing a perfect impression of the photographer-as-paparazzo, too much wine and just the right amount of impropriety causing Kate to double over, shaking with laughter until her stomach hurt. He always did know how to crack her up, like a secret key that only he knew how to find.

"Now, a lesser couple might have seen some bad omens here and gone running, but Kate and I, we're made of tougher stuff than that. A wedding is just one day, but a marriage is a life's work, something you're constantly building and growing and expanding." He turns to the young couple. "Your marriage will be the foundation of your family, of your life, and if you put the work in to build it solid—to make it tough, so to speak—it'll hold you up in good times and in bad."

Kate looks up at Bruce, a little balder, a lot greyer, with a bit of a pot belly, but still the Bruce of their wedding day. She remembers she meant to write out a list that morning, all those years ago, of what she loved about him, so she'd never forget. She hadn't gotten around to it—too many details, too much to do—but the twinkle in those blue eyes is all the reminder she needs. It was his kindness and his sense of humour. The way he always opened her car door before his own. The way he teared up when his mother called to let him know his dog had passed away. The way he danced in the mornings while waiting for the coffee maker, sweeping her into his arms despite her pre-caffeine crankiness, making her smile.

"I've been lucky enough to have been married for twenty-eight years to a woman who is kind and loyal, and smart, sometimes cranky and often persnickety—"

Kate shakes her fist at him, but she can't help grinning.

"... and who puts up with my complete lack of interest in home improvement. She's the one who takes care of our whole family, but most of all, this lovely, generous, sweet young lady in white up here today."

Kate looks over at her daughter watching Bruce with rapt attention, holding hands with her new husband. It's a lovely wedding, a perfect wedding. Her daughter is ready for something new. And, to her surprise, Kate realizes she is ready for something old. Something as familiar as an old shoe, a rhythm that echoes in her memory, a rediscovering of a time long past. To be part of a couple, not just Mom and Dad but Kate and Bruce. Tomorrow, they'll go out for breakfast, she thinks. Maybe talk about a trip. Plan. Organize. Dream.

"Now, it's time for the two of you to take care of each other. We're going to miss having our Little Miss Sunshine around to laugh indulgently at my jokes and make pies for Sunday dinner. But I'd like to think that instead of making a crack in our foundation, we're adding an extra layer of support. Some more insulation, perhaps, a son-in-law shaped coating of protection against future troubles."

It's been a long goodbye, parenthood. Well, maybe not goodbye—just a bittersweet farewell to how things were. Time for a hello to how things are going to be. Kate's ready.

"So, welcome to the family, and may your marriage be strong, multiplied by the love of generations past."

The room breaks into warm applause as Bruce walks over to the head table and kisses his daughter on the cheek, shakes hands with the groom. Then he turns to Kate and winks in that old familiar way. Kate wipes at her eyes—thank heavens the photos are already done—and feels something bubble up inside, something exceptional, something precious. She knows what it is.

Joy.

At the head table, the bride whispers something to Bruce, then he returns to the microphone.

"I've been asked to announce a bit of housekeeping. The person at each table with the purple dot under their side plate can take home the centrepiece. Thanks."

Bruce returns to the table to find Kate dabbing fresh tears with her napkin and gives her a tender smile as he slides into his seat. He slips an arm around her shoulders, pulling her in. "It's okay, honey—she'll always be our baby."

Kate blots at her face and takes a deep breath. "No, it's not that... it's just that... I really wanted the centrepiece!"

He laughs, seeing that the pastor across the table looks pleased as punch with his little vase of salmon carnations. Bruce looks down at her with a familiar, bemused smile, his special Kate smile, the one that lets her know she isn't fooling him. He knows her, knows the truth. "Please tell me I get to kiss you right now."

She puffs out a little snort and wipes the tears away. "You old fool," she says, but leans in, lips and heart and dreams at the ready.

Casey at the Wedding

ood evening everyone, I'm Casey.

I'd like to start by saying this to the groom: I'm sorry.

While I may be your Best Man, it seems I have not always been the Best Brother.

Imagine, if you will, two young boys, more twins than brothers, although one is a year older. The older, blonder one with the great hair convinces the younger, darker one with the shy eyes that it sure would be cool to go down to the swampy pond that had formed one spring in the empty lot a few houses down, maybe catch some frogs, maybe make a mud tower. So, they head out, with their dad's good fishing net, and to their delight, when they arrive there are tadpoles in the water. They wade out, a bit more, a bit more, scoop a few tadpoles into a jar, then it's time to go home.

Only there's trouble—the younger one is stuck—like he's standing in cement, his feet encased, can't move at all, and he panics and drops the fishing net into the depths from which it will never be recovered. And the older one—in absolute, honest belief, I swear—starts screaming, "Quicksand! Quicksand!" And the younger one cries, thinking he has mere moments to live. Then, the older one, having reached the limit of his supervisory capabilities, makes a break for home to get help, only the younger one thinks he's being abandoned to the quicksand, and, probably, alligators and piranhas.

So, in tears and terror, he pulls his feet right out of his rubber boots and squelches through the mud, flapping home in smelly, wet socks, bawling the whole way, like a baby swamp-monster looking for his mom.

You know, I think we were both expecting a warmer welcome at home, considering we'd narrowly escaped death and all.

So, I'm sorry about that incident, Little Bro. I take full responsibility, and in all fairness, I probably owe you a week's dessert. But while we're talking about the times I was a less-than-perfect brother, there's a few other things I'd like to apologize for as well.

I'm sorry I hit you in the head that time with a Fisher Price toy camera, and you had to get stitches.

Although, in my defense, I was aiming at Mr. Rogers who was on the TV behind you. I always hated that guy.

I'm sorry that when we used to play Super Friends with the neighbourhood kids, I always got to be Superman while you had to be Aquaman. Although, you were eerily good at making dolphin sounds. EEE. EEE. Anyway, I apologize.

Sorry about the nightmares—I always felt somewhat responsible because I let you watch *Aliens* when I was babysitting for the first time, even though your late-night ramblings seem to imply they were about being smothered by dandelions. But I like to think I made up for it by letting you sleep in my bed any time you wanted. Despite the kicking. You're welcome.

I'm sorry I always got to be the one to pick out shirts and pants, and you had to wear my hand-me-downs, meaning you spent some of your key formative years in shirts featuring farting donkeys and an awful lot of track pants. At least you had the sense not to wear them for school picture day. Unlike someone else I know. Sorry, Mom!

I'm really sorry about that one time when you were in fourth grade, and you were trying really hard to impress a cute girl in your class, so you told her you had a robot in your bedroom that cleaned it for you, and she came to me for validation, and I failed to back you up.

Sorry I just told the world about that robot thing.

I apologize for that one time that Gramma and Gramps brought us back pocket knives as gifts from a trip to Spain, and I cried because you got the black-handled one and I got the brown-handled one, but I wanted the black one, and you caved in and traded with me. You have a good heart. I was—am—a whiny baby.

Also... sorry for using your hair as a tester for my new black-handled knife.

I'm sorry for the time when Mom was on the evening shift, and it was just you and me at home, and your hamster had an end-of-life event. I just didn't know how to make it all better, dude—I didn't know what to say. I did the best I could, and I hope it was enough. And you have to admit, I throw one hell of a hamster funeral.

I'm sorry for that one time you came to visit me in San Francisco, while I was on a work term out there, and my buddies and I took you out for one too many Long Island Iced Teas, and while you were passed out we put a temporary tattoo of Hello Kitty on your arm. When you woke up we told you it was real, and you believed us for a full eight hours before it began to wash off.

Actually, never mind, that was hilarious—would do again.

Okay. Deep breath—this is a tough one.

I'm sorry that when Dad got sick, I wasn't there for you more. I know I was away by then, but I still regret not coming home to, I don't know, be helpful or be serious or be funny or just be *there*. I was scared and sad, and I left you to battle through on your own. It wasn't good for either of us, and if I could have one do-over, just one, this would be it.

Being a good brother is hard. But this guy up here, he never had any trouble with it. He's the one you turn to when you need to borrow a few bucks to make it through to pay day. He's the one you know will give the perfect toast at Christmas dinner. He's the one who will help you move and expertly tip the movers, all the while never asking why this is your third move in six months. He's the one who quietly shows up at your place with a six-pack and a suggestion to watch the game together, when your love life has fallen into ruin, again, and who will never, ever make a Mighty Casey striking out joke.

He's a catch—but sorry ladies, he's found someone who, magically, is just as good as he is. Who is caring and smart and loyal. So, I'm sorry, you all will have to settle for me—the line forms to the left.

I can offer you great hair, really solid apologies, and a ticket into the best family I know.

So, let's all raise our glasses to the bride and groom. May they truly understand that love does mean having to say you're sorry, although I think these two won't have to say it too often—at least not as often as I do. Here's to love and laughter and happily ever after!

Willow at the Wedding

*O*h. My. God. It is totally going to happen. I spent like, most of last night picturing it happening because Taylor says that if you envision something, it actually will happen. You just need to really see it in your mind, so I did, and it was like it was really happening. Just you wait.

That bouquet will be mine. It's destiny. And when I catch it, love will be mine, too, because that's how it works, and you don't mess around with the wedding gods, if you know what's good for you.

I've been thinking, of course, about Fletcher and how he is, like, so cute. The other day at work he leaned over and said *how long have these been in the fryer,* and I noticed for the first time he has exactly four freckles on the left side of his nose—my left, so his right, I guess—in a diamond pattern, and it seemed like, I don't know, maybe a birthmark?

Because who has freckles exactly like that, right? I will have to check his younger brother for the same ones if I see him coming in with the team after baseball practice. Although, I will have to be clever about it because if he sees me checking him out, and then I end up with Fletcher, it is going to be just so weird at every Christmas dinner, not to mention our own wedding, which will be as pretty as this one, for sure.

I am so excited about my present! It stands right out on the table of gifts over there because I splurged on this amazing glossy paper with roses, plus a matching bow and everything. My mom said, *I'm getting them a place setting, just put your name on it*, but a) place settings are lame, like, you're just one sheep in the heard, know what I mean, and b) I wanted to give them something just from me because, hello, Junior Bridesmaid and all. So, I went to the mall and guess what I found? Socks! The cutest things—hers are purple with unicorns on them, knee socks, and his are like dress socks in yellow, but not a gross yellow, a nice bright yellow with bacon strips on them. Bacon! And they were on for buy two, get one free, so I got myself some totally awesome rainbow socks with—get this—toes in them, and I love them, and the future Mr. Willow better love them, too, because I think I will wear them to my own wedding, under my dress. How cool would that be?

I think Fletcher would be into it.

The most unbelievable thing happened last weekend. I was working the seven-to-seven shift on Saturday—I still haven't gotten a new shirt, BTW, I know mine is stained with ketchup, but I just can't bring myself to spend another forty bucks on a brown polyester frightfest. Like, they need to revamp the uniforms, stat. Plus, I am totally going to be down, like, fifteen pounds by the time school starts. Anyway, I was on drive-thru and who do you think comes by? Keith, driving with Ayesha in the front seat, and you know they knew I'd be there. All cozy with each other—Ayesha wasn't even wearing a seatbelt—and she gave me such a look, I just froze and stood there with their change in my hand forever, until Keith had to say *hey can you give me my change or what*, like, how embarrassing. I just know she's the one who started the rumours about me last winter, because I mean, who else benefitted, right? She's with Keith, now, is all I'm saying, so she wound up on the plus side while I'm standing there with two-seventy-five in my hand and a broken heart and my mouth hanging open like a dead fish. I couldn't do much more than push up my glasses and hand over the money and hope he didn't notice the zit on my forehead, which, of course, showed up that morning. Ugh, it kills me that he still looks so good. In a just world, he'd have warts and be thirty pounds heavier by now. Don't tell anyone, but I gave Ayesha a real Coke instead of a diet Coke. It's the little things, you know?

I'm totally grooving on my hair today. It's growing in really well since I let Taylor have a whack at it in the spring, like, that's a mistake I'll never repeat, breakup or no breakup. And now that it's a few inches longer, my mom curled it into these little swirls, and I even have—get this—a tiara! I know, I know, it's juvenile, but it just makes me feel so pretty. I'm like Princess Willow! Bow before me! I will receive you now!

Man, weddings are so great. Love is in the air!

I wish I'd had the nerve to invite Fletcher, but I guess I would have been too busy with wedding stuff to be a good date, anyway. You know what I like best about him? Okay, besides the red hair, I kind of have a thing for that. It's that he's new. No history, a total mystery. Different school and everything. I mean, it's only been a couple of months since he moved here, but I can tell the guy has depth. The great thing, though, is that we don't have to talk about it, to know all the details. We can just look at each other and *feel.* He brushed my hand the other day when we were packing the same takeout order, and there were *tingles*. And I'm pretty sure it was on purpose.

New is what I need. A fresh start. A reset.

The wedding cake is divine; it's that red chocolate thing, I think. Anyway, it totally melts in your mouth, and I will totally be getting a wedding cake for every birthday for the rest of my life, now. Princess Willow commands it! I already had a second piece. One last hurrah because I am going to start a new diet on Monday. This cake is a pretty good way to go out, I say. Of course, I got a little bit of chocolate filling on the hem of my dress. Is there anything I own that isn't stained? Sigh. But I don't think anyone will notice; the light in here is pretty dim, and the flowers around the edge of the skirt really mask it. The groom's brother said he is going to ask me to dance, and I laughed because he is like, super old. But if he does ask I guess I will say yes because it's a wedding, and I've had cake, and there is love in the air. It's so romantic!

God, I just love a wedding. They're like the ultimate happy ending, right? It's like, the very definition of hope. White dresses and flowers and cake and hope. We can all make it, too, we just need to hang in there. Did you know that the bride met the groom the day after she graduated from high school? I've seen them together at every family reunion for like, eight years. I figure my Mr. Right could be anywhere, just around the corner, like maybe I know him right now. I have a strong feeling Fletcher is going to ask me out, maybe next week or the week after. Or maybe I will, because it's modern times and all that, and if I catch the bouquet—when I catch it— it is certain to be some kind of sign. Don't mess with the wedding gods, right? If we can only make it through to graduation, I know we'll make it all the way to the happy ending—I can just feel it.

I should call him. Right? Maybe tonight or maybe tomorrow. Or Monday because a lot of people are busy on the weekend. I can ask him about the shifts for next week and hint around that the new *Avengers* movie looks really good. I'll let the wedding gods decide, I think. They seem to know what they're doing.

There's the bride, now, coming to the middle of the dance floor, and she's got her flowers in her hand. A mix of wildflowers, carnations too, looks like; I would have gone with roses myself, but it'll do. It's my big moment. I'm going to be at the front of the pack. Although, something tells me it doesn't matter where I stand because I'm ready for love, and it's going to find me. Oh, yes it is. I've got both hands open, and I'm a great catch, so bring it on—I'm ready.

ABOUT THE AUTHOR

Lynn Jatania is an author of fiction and non-fiction from Ottawa, Ontario. *Ten at the Wedding* is her first published book.

Follow her blog at
lynnjatania.com

THANK YOU CARDS

Thanks to my sisters in writing, authors Lee Ann Eckhardt Smith and Jennifer Roundell–you both know I wouldn't be where I am today without you.

Thanks to my self-published author inspirations, Tudor Robins and Catherine Brunelle, for all your kind advice.

Thanks to Beth Beasley and her enduringly positive and delightful writing classes–you make me feel like a real writer.

Thanks to my beta reader, Marnie, for your valuable input and thoughtful comments.

Thanks to my editor, Jennifer Jaquith of Morning Rain Publishing, and cover designer, Vivian Cheng of Blend Creations, both of whom made this book so much better.

Thanks to my family–Neel, Arjun, Nisha, and Kiran–for your indulgence and support, and for being my own favourite dinner party guests.